D0613148

The ITTY·BITTY KIDDIES Wake Up

Written by
H. I. Peeples

Illustrated by
Michael Montgomery

A CALICO BOOK
Published by Contemporary Books, Inc.
CHICAGO · NEW YORK

Library of Congress Cataloging-in-Publication Data
Peeples, H. I.
The Itty-Bitty Kiddies wake up / written by H. I. Peeples :
illustrated by Michael Montgomery.
p.   cm.
"A Calico book."
Summary: Before going out to play, a young boy's small friends make a
mess bathing, brushing their teeth, dressing, and eating breakfast.
ISBN 0-8092-4345-8
[1. Cats—Fiction.   2. Stories in rhyme.]   I. Montgomery,
Michael, 1952–   ill.   II. Title.
PZ8.3.P27636It   1989
[E]—dc19   89-1247
                                                                  CIP
                                                                  AC

Copyright © 1990 by The Kipling Press
Text copyright © 1990 by James Conrad
Illustrations copyright © 1990 by Michael Montgomery
Designed by Tilman Reitzle
All rights reserved
Published by Contemporary Books, Inc.
180 North Michigan Avenue, Chicago, Illinois 60601
Manufactured in the United States of America
International Standard Book Number: 0-8092-4345-8

Published simultaneously in Canada by Beaverbooks, Ltd.
195 Allstate Parkway, Valleywood Business Park
Markham, Ontario L3R 4T8 Canada

Jerry was just like other boys
But for the secret inside his shoe.
Five Itty-Bitty Kiddies slept in there,
And they were quite a playful crew.

Bitsy and Bumble woke up first
And jumped up onto Jerry's bed.
Tiny woke next but not to play—
Breakfast was on his mind instead.

Next Itsy woke to take control
And lead the others in their play.
She roused Teeny with a whistle
So that she wouldn't sleep all day.

Now Itsy lined the Kiddies up
And found a feather for a plume.
She used a thimble for a drum
And marched them out of Jerry's room

6

When noise poured through the bathroom door,
Jerry sat up and rubbed his eyes.
He thought the Kiddies were washing up—
He was in for a big surprise.

The sink had been filled by Bitsy,
Who was now trying to impress
The others with his diving skills.
He scored high marks but made a mess!

Tiny jumped upon the toothpaste tube
And landed squarely with both feet.
Toothpaste flew into his mouth.
He found it was no breakfast treat!

9

Bumble had found the dental floss
And stretched a tightrope way up high.
Even Itsy could not resist
And wanted to give it a try.

She felt as if she walked on air
'Til Bumble began to crowd her.
She missed a step, and down she fell
Right into a box of powder.

The powder settled down like snow,
Leaving Itsy covered all in white.
Then suddenly she found herself
In the middle of a powder fight.

Jerry finally broke it up:
"This isn't what you all should do!"
And added (counting only four),
"I thought that there were *five* of you."

Teeny, who never made a sound,
Had been forgotten in the rush.
She was so shy that Jerry found
Her in the bristles of his brush.

"I'll show you how to wash and dress."
With all the Kiddies gathered near,
Jerry lathered his hands and face.
He even scrubbed behind each ear.

And when it was the Kiddies' turn,
They soon learned washing could be fun.
They ran their hands across the soap
And did just what their friend had done.

Jerry put the toothpaste on his brush
And scrubbed up top and down beneath.
Then Jerry showed how dental floss
Removes what's left between your teeth.

Due to the Kiddies' smaller size,
They found themselves at quite a loss.
So all used cotton swabs to brush
And tiny thread for dental floss.

17

As Jerry brushed his hair he thought
His brush was much too large to share.
So he got out a new toothbrush
With which all five could brush their hair.

Into toy cars the Kiddies hopped
And sped across the bedroom floor.
Jerry put them in their dressing rooms;
Each Kiddy had a dresser drawer.

The minute Bumble was alone,
He pulled his clothes down from their pegs.
He put his arms inside his pants
And wore his shirtsleeves on his legs!

When Jerry saw what Bumble'd done,
He helped him dress the proper way.
Now everyone was dressed and clean
And could go out to run and play.

But Jerry noticed, once again,
That the five Kids were down to four.
Somehow a lone Itty-Bitty
Had slipped beneath the bedroom door.

Then from the kitchen came a crash,
Sending them all running that way.
It was Tiny who'd remembered
Breakfast's the way to start each day!